Disney • HYPERION

Cooper's Big-Kid Day

Written by Calliope Glass   Illustrated by Mike Wall

"Come on, Mommy!" Cooper called from the front door. "Let's go, let's go, let's go!"

Cooper stomped his foot impatiently. Today was the big day. He was going to start to learn to use the potty!

Cooper and his mom were going to the store to buy some special big-kid things just for him! He couldn't wait!

"I'm coming," Cooper's mom called. "I just need to find the list."

"It's right here, Mommy!" Cooper said, waving around a sheet of paper. "Now can we go?"

Cooper's mom smiled as she grabbed her keys. "You bet!" she said, and opened the front door.

Cooper was a big kid. He did lots of big-kid things. He brushed his teeth and cleaned up his toys before bed. He even picked out his own clothes.

"How'd you get to be so big?" Cooper's mom asked as she buckled him into his car seat. "You used to be small enough for me to carry in one arm!"

"Moooom," Cooper said. "That's when I was a baby. I'm all grown up now!"

Cooper's mom smiled down at him. "You may be a big kid now, but you'll always be my baby," she said.

When Cooper was a baby, he drank from a bottle, he slept in a crib, and he pooped and peed in his diaper. His mom and dad would change his diaper whenever it was wet or dirty. They even wiped him clean, because he was too small to do it himself.

Now Cooper was a big boy. He slept in a big boy bed, he wore training pants, and he ate dinner all by himself. He was tall, he was strong, he was smart—and he was ready to use the toilet!

"I can't wait to have my own potty!" Cooper told his mom as they drove to the store.

Cooper and his mom were buying everything Cooper needed for potty training.

"I want to pick everything myself!" Cooper said. "Can I?"

"You sure can," Cooper's mom said, smiling at him in the rearview mirror.

"Yay!" Cooper shouted. "Are we almost there?"

"A little longer," Cooper's mom said. "Why don't you tell me what's on the list?"

Cooper happily held up the sheet of paper. "We need a potty," he said, "and training pants!"

Cooper's mom nodded. "And what else?" she asked.

"Stickers!" Cooper said. "Stickers, stickers, stickers!" He waved his Mickey doll around, making it do a little sticker dance.

Finally, Cooper and his mom got to the store. Cooper looked at all the potties. There were so many to choose from. Some of them were big, and some were smaller. There was a blue one and a pink one and a green one.

At the end of the row, Cooper found the one he wanted. It had his favorite character, Mickey Mouse, on it. "That one! That one!" he said, happily dancing around.

"What's next?" Cooper's mom asked.

Cooper looked at his list again. "Stickers!" he said.

Cooper took a long time to decide. He liked the stickers with flowers and the stickers with fish. But the star stickers were his favorite.

"Mommy, look!" Cooper said. "Can we get these?"

"You're the boss," Cooper's mom said, putting the stickers in their cart.

There was just one thing left to buy: training pants. Cooper had no trouble picking the ones he wanted!

Back at home, Cooper couldn't wait to use his new potty. He was ready to be a big kid!

Cooper and his mom went online and printed out a rewards chart. Then they took the chart and the potty into the bathroom.

"Come oooon!" Cooper whined as his mom got the potty out of the package and set it up. But when he sat down, nothing happened.

Cooper and his mom tried to pass the time by reading a book. But he still didn't have to go. "It's okay," his mom said, ruffling his hair. "Why don't we get you a pair of your new training pants? Then you can go play with your toys. You can try to use the potty again later."

Cooper nodded and followed his mom to his room. As he put on his training pants, he looked at himself in the mirror. Cooper grinned. Now he really felt like a big kid.

Cooper pulled on his pants and ran to the living room to play with his cars. Soon his dad came home.

"Hey, bud!" he said. "Whatcha doing?"

"Waiting to go potty," Cooper said.

Cooper's dad sat down next to him. "How about if I keep you company, huh? And when you're ready to go, you just let me know, okay?"

Cooper nodded as he pushed his red car around the track. "Okay!"

Soon Cooper and his dad were racing their cars around the room. Cooper was having so much fun that he forgot all about using the potty. He didn't realize he had to pee until it was too late.

"Oh, no!" Cooper said. He was really upset. "I wet my training pants."

Cooper's dad gave him a hug and helped him change into clean training pants. "It's okay, buddy," he said. "Accidents happen. We'll try again later."

Cooper nodded and went back to the living room to play with his cars some more. He tried to pay attention to how his body felt so he would notice the next time he had to pee.

Cars

Training Pants

Cooper was pushing his blue car around the room when he felt something low in his belly. He had to pee!

"Mommy!" Cooper yelled. He ran toward the bathroom. "Mommy, I have to pee!"

Cooper pulled down his pants and his training pants and sat down on the potty. Soon he was peeing . . . all by himself!

"Good job, Cooper," his mom said. "I'm so proud of you!"

Cooper's mom helped him wipe off and wash his hands in the sink.

Cooper was proud of himself, too. He dried his hands and then pointed at his chart. "Can I do the sticker now?" he asked.

Cooper carefully peeled off a sticker and stuck it to his chart. "Look, Mommy!" he said. "My first star! I'm going to get lots and lots of stars."

Cooper's mom smiled at him. "You bet you are," she said, putting her arm around him. "After all, you're a big kid now!"

Become a *Big-Kid* like Cooper

With an underwear-like fit and outstanding protection, Pull-Ups® can help make potty training as fun for your child as it was for Cooper! Whether it's advice, support, or fun activities, we have everything you need to make your training journey a memorable one.

coopers toys

Keep the potty going with Pull-Ups®

We're here to help you and your Big Kid throughout your entire journey. Visit **pull-ups.com** for more helpful tips, fun games, and informational resources.